Aly Cat

TAKES OVER
FIRST GRADE!

BY **ELLEN LEROE**

ILLUSTRATED BY
TOM LABAFF

SCHOLASTIC INC.
NEW YORK TORONTO LONDON AUCKLAND SYDNEY
MEXICO CITY NEW DELHI HONG KONG BUENOS AIRES

Dedicated with love to Iris and Elma: the original spunky girls
—E.L.

ISBN-13: 978-0-545-08527-4
ISBN-10: 0-545-08527-6

12 11 10 9 8 7 6 5 4   9 10 11 12 13/0

Printed in the U.S.A.
First printing, November 2008

FIRST GRADE JITTERS

This morning I got up in the dark. I put a finger to my lips to shush Einstein. He's my super-smart goldfish.

I grabbed Mr. Jaws, my new battery-operated toy shark. Then I tippy-slippy-toed into the hall and into Giraffe Girl's room. In case you Nosy Rosies need to know, Giraffe Girl is my thirteen-year-old sister, Merry.

I held my breath and pushed the door open. Giraffe Girl looked like a big rock under her covers. I crept into her closet and quietly shut the door. I held on to Mr. Jaws, extra tight. I smiled a poison-ivy-smile in the dark.

When my sister finally opened the closet door, I pushed the shark into her face. I pressed his button. Chomp! Chomp! Chomp!

Giraffe Girl threw up her hands and screamed, "Alyssa Catherine, you little monster!"

"Gotcha!" I said. Before she could grab me, I wiggled away. I doggy-paddled my way downstairs and swam into the kitchen with my shark.

I sat down at the table. Mr. Jaws sat down, too, right in the middle of my plate.

"Ready for your super special breakfast?" Mom asked.

NEWS FLASH! Today is the first day of school. Good-bye, kindergarten! Hello, first grade!

Mom turned from the stove.

"No fish allowed on the table. Remember our rule?"

My sister came in. She is tall and skinny. Hot rollers covered her head.

"How about no giraffes allowed?" I asked.

Merry rolled her eyes and sat down.

"Funneeee."

She blew on her wet nails.

"Remember, three for me," I told my mom.

I moved Mr. Jaws onto my lap. I picked up the maple syrup. Scaring my older sister made me really hungry. Mom slid three pancakes onto my plate.

"How come she gets three and I get two?" Merry asked.

" 'Cause I eat one pancake for the start of each new school grade starting from kindergarten *and* one for good luck," I explained.

"When you're a senior in high school, are you going to eat fourteen pancakes?"

"Mom will make mine itty-bitty," I said.

"You should come with a warning label," Merry mumbled in between bites.

She pointed her fork at me.

"You're something else."

"What else?" I asked. "Something good?"

She gave me a long look.

"Sometimes," she said.

And then she smiled. I smiled back.

Dad hurried into the kitchen. He looked at his watch.

"Time to get crack-a-lackin'," he said.

I finished breakfast and ran upstairs to get dressed.

When I came back down, Mom froze.

"I hope you're not thinking of wearing those flippers to school," she said.

"Why not?" I looked down at my feet.

"Because you're going to school, not the pool!
Now go upstairs and put on shoes."

Mom crossed her arms and waited.

I gave a great big Aly Cat sigh. Then I flapped
my way back up the steps. I huffed and puffed all
the way.

I hurried downstairs.

Mom stared at my feet and smiled. She hugged

me and said, "Try not to be a handful, okay?"

"I'll try," I said. *But I can't promise*, I thought.

Dad drove me to Dailey Elementary. I saw my friends in the playground. I jumped out of the car. Dad leaned out the window and smiled at me.

"Have fun, Aly Cat Cutie," he said very loudly.

Then he drove away. I heard laughing behind me. I felt a poke.

"Aly Cat Cutie!" Aidan Cherkas shouted when I turned around.

"Or is Cootie your last name?"

Aidan Cherkas always has something rude or gross to say. He and his buddy, Sean Rufus the Doofus, laughed loudly.

"It's Alyssa Catherine Anderson, and you know it!"

I put my hands on my hips. I frowned.

"No, it's not," Aidan shouted. "It's Cootie! Your dad just said it. You're Aly Cat Cootie!"

"Cootie Cat," Sean added.

Holy Moldy Bananas.

I squeezed my eyes shut. I wished I could go home.

"Aly Cat Cootie!" Aidan sang. "Aly the Cootie Cat!"

I opened my eyes.

"Don't say that!" I warned in my most itchy-scritchy spider voice.

"Sure, Cootie Cat!" Aidan yelled. "We won't say it!"

He and Sean ran around me. They were screeching like monkeys.

"Aly Cat Cootie! Aly Cat Cootie!"

The bell rang, and they ran inside. I stood there with my hands in fists. I tried not to cry.

Purple Pooper Scoopers! What a bumpy, down-in-the-dumpy day!

WORDY BIRDY

"Aly Cat, over here!"

My best friend Brittany waved to me. She stood just inside our classroom. Last week we had visited 1B and met our teacher, Ms. Spangler. We had also met our furry class rat, named Jupiter.

Ms. Spangler came out into the hallway. I loved her sunny gold hair and blue glasses with tiny sparkles.

"Hello, Aly," Ms. Spangler said with a big smile. "Why don't you go inside and find your seat? There's a goody bag with your name on it."

I tugged on Britt's arm.

"Are we sitting near the windows this year?"

Brittany made a little face.

"We're not at the same table."

"What? But we always sit together. We do *everything* together. That's why we're called the Stick-Like-Glue Two."

"Ms. Spangler put me near Jupiter's cage," Britt said. "I want to be able to watch him."

"Whoa," I said, kind of huffy. "Who's more important, the class rat or your best friend?"

"I don't want to switch seats," Britt said. "Don't be mad."

My icky mood went dippy. It got worse when I found my seat. Guess who my three other table partners turned out to be? Sean, Max (a boy who picks his nose), and Deloris, Miss Know-It-All. That Deloris is a pain in the brain.

"Class, hang up your backpacks," Ms. Spangler said. "Put your goody bags away and come to the rug. I have a special book to read."

I ran over to sit next to Brittany but a girl named Hannah plopped down next to her. I tapped Hannah on the shoulder and nicely asked her to move. That didn't work.

I gave her my spinach stare, all mean, green, and yucky. Hannah still didn't move. Luckily, my other bestest friend Miguel sat down next to me.

"Hola," he said.

He likes to speak Spanish sometimes.

"HOLA, MY NEW BEST FRIEND," I said in an extra-loud voice.

I wanted Britt to hear.

"Sshhh," Deloris said. "You're too loud."

"You sshhh yourself," I whippy-snipped back.

Ms. Spangler looked over.

"Who's being a Wordy Bird during story time?"

Deloris pointed at me.

"Aly's the Wordy Bird. She's blabbing."

I jumped up.

"I am not! You're the Wordy Bird, Deloris! You started it."

"No, *you* did!" Deloris yelled.

"Girls," Ms. Spangler said.

Her smile froze a little.

"Well, if I'm a Wordy Birdy," I told Deloris, "then you're a Yucky Ducky!"

Miguel laughed. So did the other kids.

Aidan turned around and looked up at me.

"Look who's talking, Aly Cat Cootie."

More kids laughed. My face burned. I didn't like that. Ms. Spangler clapped her hands. Sharpish.

"Alyssa Catherine! Please sit down."

I made a shark smile at Deloris and sat down.

Ms. Spangler read us a book called *Chrysanthemum* about a girl mouse with a funny name.

Ms. Spangler closed the book.

"Let's talk about people's names."

Deloris shot a hand in the air.

"Chrysanthemum is a dumb name. Deloris is a super deluxe name!"

"Deloris Brontosaurus," I said in a loud whisper.

Miguel laughed. So did Brittany and the girl next to her.

"I heard that," Deloris snapped.

Her face got all red.

"Wordy Birdy's talking again!"

Ms. Spangler gave a little sigh. She held up the book.

"All names are special in this class, just like Chrysanthemum," she said. "Let's make believe we're Nice Mice. Do you know what Nice Mice do?"

We shook our heads.

"Nice Mice don't call one another names that hurt," Ms. Spangler said. "They are nice to their classmates."

I did a little wiggle. I couldn't look at Deloris.

"Raise your hand if you think you can be Nice Mice," Ms. Spangler said.

She raised her hand. More hands went up. My hand crept up. Slowish. I peeked over at Deloris. How could I be nice to a pain in the brain like that?

Then Ms. Spangler talked about class rules.

She helped us put our supplies away. Then she clapped her hands.

"Let's make a circle on the rug, legs crossed," she said.

I quickly jumped up and sat next to Brittany. Miguel sat on my other side.

"Boys and girls, follow what I do," Ms. Spangler said.

She began to pat, pat her knee, then clap her hands once.

Pat, pat, clap. Pat, pat, clap.

"Let's take turns," Ms. Spangler said.

"Say your first name, and something you like that starts with the same letter as your name."

Ms. Spangler pat, patted her knee, and clapped her hands.

"My name is Ms. Spangler and I like swimming."

Miguel said "motorcycles." Then it was my turn.

Pat, pat, clap. Pat, pat, clap.

I couldn't think of anything. Then I did.

"My name is Aly and I like April fourth for Brittany's birthday."

Britt looked at me and grinned.

She said, "My name is Brittany and I like bubble gum."

Sean said "scary movies." Deloris said "dogs." I never knew she liked dogs. Then it was Aidan's turn.

I leaned over to Brittany.

"Bet he says A for anything awful."

We giggled, waiting.

"My name is Aidan and I like art," he said.

I quick took a shocked breath. Never in a million years did I think he would say that. But then he made a horrible noise. Some of the boys laughed. Brittany and I rolled our eyes. Aidan Cherkas was still disgusting.

BiG ANNOUNCEMENT

When I got home from school, Grandma Elma was waiting for me. She gave me a big kiss and hug and a little tap on the top of my head. Then she called me her funny peanut. We sat in the kitchen. I told her about my first day of school and my problems. That Britt wouldn't change her seat to sit next to me. And that pain in the brain Deloris got me into trouble at story time. And Aidan called me Aly Cat Cootie and everyone laughed.

"School is going to get better," Grandma Elma promised me. "You'll see."

The next day, **NEWS FLASH!** She was right! Ms. Spangler made a special announcement after the Pledge of Allegiance.

"Boys and girls, next Friday we're getting a new student," she said. "Her name is Gilana Samuel. She and her family come from the West Indies island of St. Lucia. Does anyone know where that is?"

"Is that in India?" Max asked.

"St. Lucia is not in India," Ms. Spangler said. She smiled and pointed to the large map.

"It's halfway between the United States and South America."

Ms. Spangler tapped on a small island on the map.

"This area is called the West Indies, or the Caribbean," she explained.

Ms. Spangler turned on the TV in the front of the room. She played a video for us. It was about the island of St. Lucia.

Let me tell you, it was more beautiful than my sister's sparkly beaded purse! There were colorful beaches with green water, palm trees, and a big rain forest. There were two tall mountains called the Twin Pitons. The neatest thing of all was a drive-in volcano!

"Would it be fun to learn more about this island?" Ms. Spangler asked.

"Yay!" some of us shouted.

Other kids clapped. We were all excited.

"You're going to work in pairs on a project to make our new student feel at home," Ms. Spangler said. "I want you to learn more about St. Lucia. Each pair will get to pick an interesting thing about the island."

I wanted to be Brittany's partner.

"Each pair will give a short oral report, with pictures, on Friday," Ms. Spangler said. "That's when Gilana arrives."

Ms. Spangler wrote a list of things that came from St. Lucia on the board. She used different color chalks for each subject. Then she read the list out loud. As soon as she read "dolphin," I waved my hand in the air.

"Britt and I want dolphins!" I said, all excited. "We went to the big aquarium this summer and saw them!"

"Who says you get to pick first?" Deloris demanded. "I should get dolphin because it starts with D, just like my name."

"D is for *Don't Think So*," I said.

"Each of you will pull crayons out of this bag," Ms. Spangler said.

She held up a paper bag.

"The color you pick will match the word on the board in the same color."

Dolphins were orange so I *had* to get that color.

"There are two crayons of each color in the bag," Ms. Spangler said. "So if you pick a blue crayon, whoever picks the other blue one will be your partner."

Uh-oh.

That meant Brittany and I both had to get orange crayons. I didn't like the sound of that.

"Who wants to go first?" Ms. Spangler asked.

"Me! Me! ME!" I shouted.

I bounced right out of my seat.

"No, pick me!" Deloris yelled.

She got up and pushed in front of me!

"You're sitting quietly, Jewel," Ms. Spangler said. "You may pick first."

"Not fair, Ms. Spangler," Deloris declared. "I

shouted the loudest."

"Students who aren't making a fuss will be picked first," Ms. Spangler said.

She frowned at Deloris—and me. I slumped in my seat. I made my mean, green spinach face at Deloris.

"Troublemaker," I muttered.

Jewel got the Piton Mountains, and **NEWS FLASH!** Jamal was her partner! Miguel and Taylor got the St. Lucia parrot called the Jacquot. Max and Fu Lin got the coral reef. Everything on the board was taken, except for the dolphin, flag, and Kouwes snake.

Then Brittany pulled out the orange crayon for dolphins. I did a victory wiggle in my seat. Sean picked white for the flag. Aidan got green for the Kouwes snake. Then it was down to

Deloris, Hannah, and me. Deloris put her hand inside the crayon bag and bumped it all around. Half of her eyeball was trying to peek inside that bag.

"No cheating!" I said.

Deloris pulled out the white crayon. She was paired with Sean to work on the flag. Hannah picked the orange crayon. Oh, no! That meant she was paired with Britt on dolphins. I reached in the bag and yucko! I pulled out the green one. Rotty Spotty Tater Tots! I was stuck with Aidan.

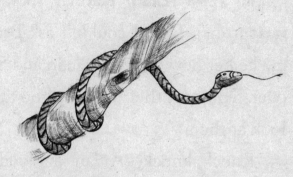

FROM BAD TO WORSE

I didn't look at Aidan for the rest of the morning. I didn't want a snake as my project, and I didn't want Aidan Cherkas Jerkus as my partner. Double Yuck times two.

The bell rang for lunch. I waited until Aidan and Sean left. I wanted to talk to Brittany about changing partners. But Hannah was with her. Hannah was always with her.

"Britt, sit with me," I shouted in the lunchroom.

But **NEWS FLASH!** Hannah took a seat right next to her. Now I couldn't ask Brittany to let me be her new partner. Aidan and Sean walked over. They put their trays on the table. I didn't look at them.

"Knock, knock," Aidan said loudly.

"Who's there?" Sean replied.

"Snot," Aidan said with a snicker.

"Snot who?" Sean asked.

"Snot nice to get paired with Aly Cat Cootie!" Aidan shouted.

I saw red. I really got mad. I grabbed Aidan's sandwich and I punched it. A fat tomato squished in two. A big blob of tuna fish dripped out. I made a hole in the middle of the bread. I gave a spinach grin.

"Oops," I said. "Aidan's got a donut sandwich."

Aidan yanked the sandwich out of my hand.

"Look what you did!" he shrieked.

Mrs. Steen, the lunchroom lady, marched over. She was one tough cookie.

"What's going on here?" she demanded.

"Aly punched my sandwich and wrecked it!" Aidan yelled.

"I didn't punch it," I said. "I maybe tapped it, hard."

Mrs. Steen looked at the sandwich. She shook her head.

"Alyssa Catherine, you'll spend recess on the bench," she said.

She turned to Aidan. "You, too."
"But—" Aidan said.

"No recess," Mrs. Steen stated.

She marched away.

"See what you did?" Aidan said.

"What *I* did?" I huffed back. "Snot nice to call me names, remember?"

I talked to Brittany alone when lunch was over.

"Can we switch partners?" I begged.

"But I'm with Hannah," she said.

"I know, but I don't want to work with Aidan!" I said.

My face burned as I thought about all the kids laughing at Cootie Cat and Aly the Cootie.

Britt chewed her lip.

"I can't, Aly. Hannah would feel bad."

"What about me?" I demanded. "Aren't I your best friend? Do you want *me* to feel bad?"

Brittany shook her head.

"Well, best friends stick together," I said. "We're the Stick-Like-Glue Two."

"But Hannah has a great DVD about dolphins," Britt said. "She's coming over to show it to me this afternoon."

I stared at her. I felt all wiggly and hot inside.

I stamped my foot.

"Forget it! Go work with your new best friend Hannah! I don't care."

"I double don't care back!" Britt shouted.

"You're not my best friend anymore, Brittany! I'm not talking to you ever again!" I said.

"Me, neither!" Britt yelled.

I kicked the wall and stomped off.

Aidan and I sat at the ends of the bench during recess. We watched all the kids playing. He gave me mean looks. I gave him meaner ones back.

Ms. Spangler asked me to come up front when we got back to the classroom. She put her arm around me and bent down.

"Aly, I heard about what happened at lunch today," she said in a low voice. "Why did you do that to Aidan's sandwich?"

"You mean, tap it?" I asked.

"What's going on?" Ms. Spangler said.

I'm no tittle-tattle squealer, but that Aidan was mean. I told Ms. Spangler all about his name-calling and the nasty knock-knock snot joke.

"And how did that make you feel?" Ms. Spangler asked.

"Bad," I said.

I tried not to cry.

Ms. Spangler sighed.

"Aly, you have a way with words. But you need to choose your words more carefully."

I did a little squirm.

"You feel bad when Aidan makes fun of you," Ms. Spangler said. "How do you think Deloris and the others feel when you make fun of them?"

"I promise I'll be better if you let me change partners," I said. "Please, Ms. Spangler, pretty please?"

"I'm sorry, Aly. I know that you and Aidan can work together just fine if you try."

I went back to my seat and sat down. I put my head on the desk and slumped over. My best friend Brittany and I were no longer talking. And I was yucky-stuck with the grossest boy in first grade as my partner.

ACTING UP

I came home in a bad mood. I tossed some stuffed animals around. I stuck out my tongue at my goldfish, Einstein. I slippy-toed into my sister's room and stole her favorite pair of shoes.

She started shouting and yelling when she couldn't find them.

I put the shoes over my ears. I crept into her

room like a dog.

"Yeow!" she screamed. "Give me back my shoes, you little monster!"

I jumped on her bed and made barking noises.

"Oh, grow up!" Merry shouted when she got them away from me.

"Oh, throw up!" I shouted back.

She slammed the door.

"Barf! Barf! Barf!" I barked outside.

Mom hurried upstairs. There was a frown on her face.

"What in the world's gotten into you?" she said. "Why are you acting up?"

"Me and Brittany aren't best friends anymore," I said in a mad voice. "And I hate the boy I have to work with in class."

"Oh," said Mom, very quiet.

"And I hate dumb snakes, too!"

I started to cry.

Mom hugged me. "I know it looks bad right now, honey. But I promise you it'll get better."

"That's what Grandma Elma said," I huffed. "And **NEWS FLASH!** It got worse."

On Monday morning Ms. Spangler handed out All About Me sheets.

"Everyone, please take these home," she said.

"Paste a photo of yourself at the top of the page and write a list of your favorite things. Turn these in by Friday so I can put them on the board."

I tried not to peek over at Brittany. I knew right off the bat the things she'd list. But, maybe she'd write different things after spending time with Hannah.

Ms. Spangler told us we were going to the library to look at books or magazines to help us with the St. Lucia project.

"What if we can't find anything?" Miguel asked.

Ms. Spangler smiled.

"Mrs. Washburn, the librarian, can help you with your projects. I told her what we're doing to welcome Gilana to our class, and she is very excited."

Ms. Spangler flicked the lights.

"Please line up with your partner at the door."

I tried to hide behind the bookcase.

"Alyssa Catherine," Ms. Spangler said, pointing. "In line with Aidan."

Aidan smiled at me. I half-smiled back. Maybe this wouldn't be so bad.

Aidan and I went right up to Mrs. Washburn when we got to the library.

"And what are you two working on?" she asked.

"The world's rarest snake," Aidan said.

I held up a card. "It's spelled K-O-U-W-E-S."

Mrs. Washburn handed Aidan the K encyclopedia. She helped him find the page with the Kouwes snake. He sat down at a back table and began reading.

Mrs. Washburn helped me find a big book on rare snakes. I took a peek inside and went *Ugh-o*. Snakes are scary. I sat down at a table with Miguel and his partner, Taylor. They were looking at a photograph of St. Lucia's national bird, the Jacquot.

Suddenly, Aidan made a noise at his table.

He stood up and made weird hiss-hiss sounds. We all turned to look at him.

"Hey, Aly," he called. "Catch!"

He threw something small and white at me. Before I could move, Britt caught it.

"It's a cow's eyeball!" Aidan yelled with a laugh.

"It's slimy!" Britt screamed.

She tossed it to Hannah. Hannah screamed, too, and dropped it. It rolled off the table and fell on the floor. Miguel bent down and picked it up.

"It's just a stupid grape that's been dipped in something white," he said.

Everyone started laughing. It was dumb, but kind of funny. I found myself giggling, too. I shouldn't have done that. Britt's face got bright red. She was embarrassed because she screamed. She glared at me.

"Now I will never talk to you for all of next year, too, Aly Cat Anderson!" she said.

She and Hannah stamped off.

Mrs. Washburn marched over to Aidan. He was going to get it, but good. But I didn't even care. Brittany was madder at me than ever, and Aidan wasn't helping with the project. He was being a big goof-off. Rotty Spotty Tater Tots! Things were getting worse and worse.

EVERYONE'S MAD AT ME!

Here's what I've learned so far about the Kouwes snake:

1) It's only found on the Maria Islands near St. Lucia.

2) It doesn't have a venom gland, so it can't poison you.

3) It's shy and comes out only at night.

I had my facts ready to share with Aidan on

Tuesday morning. Ms. Spangler told us to work in pairs on our report. Aidan and I sat at a table in back. He was drawing a fighter plane on a piece of paper.

"So what facts did you learn about the Kouwes snake?" I asked when I finished reading.

Aidan kept drawing.

"The besssst. We'll make *hiss*-tory."

I stared at him.

"Ha, ha, Cootie Cat," he said. "You're supposed to laugh. It's a joke."

"So give me your great facts," I said.

Aidan shrugged.

"You don't have anything at all?" I said. "Our report is due Friday!"

Aidan grinned.

"Don't have a cow, Cootie Cat."

"Stop calling me that!" I said in a loud voice.

Ms. Spangler turned from helping Brittany and Hannah. She frowned at us.

"Is there a problem I should know about, Aly and Aidan?" she asked.

"No problem, Ms. Spangler," Aidan said.

He turned to me and whispered, "I have an idea."

"What?" I asked.

"A good idea for the project. You'll see."

I made a growl sound under my breath.

"Listen, you're the big Wordy Birdy in this class," Aidan whispered. "So you do all the talking on Friday."

"What?" I said. "*That's* your good idea?"

"You heard me," Aidan said.

He started drawing a face on his hand.

"But that's not fair!" I said. "Why do *I* have to do all the work?"

Aidan did a little gulp. He put a frown on the hand face.

"I don't like talking in front of the class, that's why," he said in a soft voice.

I made a frowny face of my own.

"It's *still* not fair," I repeated.

"Okay, okay," Aidan said. "I'll do the pictures of the snake. Just don't make me talk."

"They better be the best and the greatest pictures," I warned him.

"They'll make *hiss*-tory," he said.

"And no more snot knock-knock jokes," I said.

He stared at me.

"Or calling me Cootie Cat," I added.

Aidan frowned and then he threw up his hands. "All right, you win."

Things were looking up! At snack time we sat on the rug. Ms. Spangler handed out granola bars to everyone.

"This is a special treat because you're all working together so well."

I had a hard time getting my wrapper off. I turned to Britt to help me. Then I remembered. She wasn't sitting next to me. She was sitting next to Hannah by the bookshelves. They were giggling.

My shoulders got all slumpy. I felt left out.

Miguel took my granola bar. He slid the paper off and handed it back.

"You should make up with Brittany," he said. "Tell her you're sorry."

"No!" I said. "She started it by not letting me be her partner. She needs to say she's sorry first."

"That's stupid," Miguel said.

"No, you're stupid!" I yelled. "You're not my friend, either!"

Miguel said something in Spanish that I didn't understand. He scooted away from me and sat next to Jamal and Jewel. My eyes felt teary. Now both my best friends were mad at me.

Holy Moldy Bananas.

PARTY, PIZZA, AND PROBLEMS

On Wednesday we worked on a banner and a poster of St. Lucia. We drew pictures of the volcano and the Twin Piton mountains. We drew pictures of the beach, the coral reef, and the rain forest.

Ms. Spangler flicked the lights to get our attention.

"The banners and poster are looking terrific,"

Ms. Spangler said. "I want everyone to stop what they're doing and put their thinking caps on. Do you have any ideas on how to make Friday more special for Gilana?"

Hands flew in the air.

"Balloons!" I shouted, waving my hand. "Like we're having a party."

"That's silly," Deloris said with a sniff. "It's not her birthday."

Britt raised her hand. "What about a Happy St. Lucia Day? We could have streamers, balloons, and decorations."

"And cake," Hannah said. "I love cake with lots of frosting!"

Everyone was bouncing in their seats. Ms. Spangler beamed.

"These are wonderful ideas!" she said. "Let

me make a list."

Happy St. Lucia Day, she wrote on the board. She added balloons, decorations, and cake.

"Anything else?" she asked.

"Pizza," Aidan called out, raising his hand.

She added pizza to the list.

"We could have this at lunchtime, right in our room!" she said. "We can do our reports right before lunch on Friday, and then have pizza and cake to celebrate. Let's thank Brittany for coming up with our Happy St. Lucia Day idea," Ms. Spangler said.

She clapped, and then the class clapped, too. Britt got all red and smiled.

But I wanted to scream. It was my idea! *I* said let's have balloons and a party! Why did Britt get to be the star? I made a growl noise under my breath. I got mad at her all over again.

On Thursday Ms. Spangler listened to us practice our reports. She walked around the room, taking us aside two by two. She handed out stars for extra good work.

Unfortunately Aidan didn't have his pictures.

"I'm afraid I can't give you and Aidan a star," Ms. Spangler said after she heard my report.

"You didn't finish it."

"It's Aidan's fault!" I told Ms. Spangler. "He didn't bring in the pictures."

Ms. Spangler sighed.

"You two have to learn how to work as a team. I just hope that you'll get your act together by tomorrow."

I dragged myself home after school.

"How was your day?" Mom asked.

I held my nose. "P.U. times two!"

I tossed my backpack on the floor and ran upstairs.

"This is a double dose of a Yucky-Ucky Day," I told Einstein.

Merry walked by my room and looked in at me. She came in.

"What's the matter with you?" she asked.

"Tomorrow's supposed to be a welcome party for the new girl, Gilana," I said in a mad voice. "Only everything stinks!"

"Like what?" Merry said.

"Aidan didn't draw the pictures of the snake for our report like he promised," I said. "We're going to get in trouble!"

"But that's not your fault," Merry said. "You did all the work."

I got teary.

"And Britt and I aren't talking and now she's friends with Hannah."

"You still haven't made up with Brittany?" Merry asked. "Why don't you write her a note?"

"That's dumb," I said.

"You miss her, don't you?" Merry said. "So telling her that won't be dumb."

"What would I say?"

"Just keep it simple," Merry said. "I'll be right back."

I hopped off the bed and ran to my desk.

I found a pretty piece of pink notepaper and got a purple pen. Purple is Britt's favorite color.

Merry came in before I sealed the envelope.

"I have something for you," she said.

She handed me a pack of dolphin stickers.

Dear Britt,
I miss you! Can we be FRIENDS AGAIN? Please Please with bubble gum on top?
-Aly ($\frac{1}{2}$ of the Stick-Like-Glue-Two) ☺

"Do you want to put these in your note to Brittany?"

I jumped up and down and hugged her.

"Thank you!" I yelled. "You're the best sister ever!"

Merry grinned at me and left.

I leaned on my dresser and stared at Einstein.

"You're super-smart," I said to my goldfish. "Now what can I do to make Miguel want to be friends again?"

I thought and thought and thought and thought. And then it hit me. I got a super fish-ilicious idea!

"Thanks, Einstein!" I said. "I just hope it works!"

SNAKES AND CAKES

On Friday I got to school extra early. The room mothers and Ms. Spangler had decorated 1B with balloons, the welcome banner, poster, and streamers. There were even giant paper palm trees by the front board!

I left the note and stickers for Brittany on top of her desk. I was nervous as I put another little note on Miguel's desk.

Then I ran up to Ms. Spangler.

"Here's my All About Me sheet."

"Thank you," she said. "I'll put it on the board with all the others."

Britt came in and opened my note.

She gave me a great big smile and rushed over to me.

"Friends again?" I asked.

"Best friends," Britt said. "The Stick-Like-Glue Two! I love my stickers!"

We hugged each other.

Then Miguel came in.

He opened the note from me and hurried over to the board. I wiggled inside as he read my All About Me sheet. I had written that being best friends with Miguel and Brittany was one of my favorite things.

Miguel smiled and pumped his fist, *yes!* I pumped mine back. Things were looking up!

I rushed over to Aidan as soon as he walked in the classroom.

"Did you bring the snake picture for the report?" I said.

"Don't have a cow," he said.

He gave me a funny smile.

"You'll see."

UH-OH. No picture meant trouble! I got a doom-and-gloomy feeling.

Ms. Spangler stood by the board and smiled at us.

"Boys and girls, take your seats. Gilana and her mother will arrive at 11:00 this morning. Please, everyone, be on your best behavior.

And let's do a nice job with our reports on St. Lucia."

Waiting all morning was hard. Finally, our principal, Ms. McBlain, entered the room with Gilana and her mother.

I stared at Gilana. She was beautiful! She had pierced ears and lots of little braids in her hair.

Gilana and her mother sat in special seats up front. They looked at the poster of St. Lucia and pointed things out to each other.

Ms. Spangler spoke quietly to them and then clapped her hands.

"Class, it's time to share your reports on St. Lucia," she said.

Deloris leaned close to me and gave me a smug smile.

"Our flag report's going to win!" she

whispered.

"It's not a contest," I said.

That girl was a real pain in the brain!

"Who wants to begin?" Ms. Spangler said.

Aidan shot two fingers in the air. That meant he had to use the bathroom. Ms. Spangler looked surprised.

"Can't this wait until we finish our reports?"

Aidan made a face and shook his head. My shoulders went all slumpy when he left the room. Was I going to have to give our snake report all alone? I didn't have any pictures or photographs to share! We started our reports.

Gilana and her mother listened carefully. Finally, only Aidan and I, and Deloris and Sean were left to give our reports. Ms. Spangler looked up at the clock and frowned.

"Aly, I'm sorry. We can't wait any longer. You'll have to start without Aidan."

I walked to the front of the room with my paper. My insides felt squeezy. Everyone else had had a partner standing next to them. I was alone.

I peeked over at Gilana and **NEWS FLASH!** She smiled right at me. Then I looked at Britt. She smiled at me, too.

"My report is on the Kouwes snake of St. Lucia," I began. "It's the rarest snake in the entire world."

I read all the facts. Just at the very end, Aidan burst in the room. I looked at him and gasped!

Ms. Spangler stared.

"Oh, my," she said in a weak voice.

Kids shouted and clapped. Aidan joined

me at the front of the room. He pointed to his face.

"This is what a Kouwes snake looks like," he said.

Aidan had painted the tail of the snake on his right cheek. The body crawled up over his right eyebrow. It slid down past his nose, and ended with the face of the snake on his lower left cheek. It was outlined in black, and the snake's tongue was bright red.

"Well," Ms. Spangler finally said. "I have to take a closer look at this."

She leaned in next to Aidan.

"I hope this paint is safe for your skin, young man."

"My mom bought it for me special," he said.

"In that case, I give you both a gold star for Most Original Project," Ms. Spangler stated.

The class clapped. Fu Lin, Sean, and Max whistled. Aidan and I returned to our seats.

Just then, surprise, surprise! The room mothers brought the pizza and a giant cake box into our room.

"My cake!" Deloris cried.

The moms put the pizza and the cake box on the back table. Ms. Spangler walked over to the table and opened the cake box.

"Oh, Deloris, this is beautiful!" Ms. Spangler cried.

I looked at Deloris.

"What's so special about the cake?"

"The frosting looks like the flag of St. Lucia," she said with a proud smile.

"I want to see!" Hannah cried.

She jumped up.

Everyone left their seats and crowded around the cake box.

"Quit pushing!" Jewel said to her brother.

"You stop!" Jamal said.

Someone bumped the box.

CRASH!

It fell off the table and hit the floor! Deloris opened the lid and stared into the box. Her lips flapped open and shut like Einstein's.

"It's all mushed up!" she yelled.

She burst into tears.

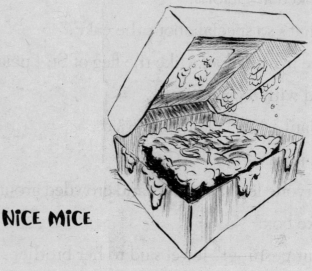

NiCE MiCE

"It's all *sploosho!*" Deloris cried.

"The cake didn't come out of the box," Ms. Spangler said in a low voice. "I'll smooth over the frosting and then we can serve it."

"But our flag is messed up!" Deloris cried.

She was crying harder now. That girl is a pain in the brain, but I felt bad for her.

"It's okay," Ms. Spangler said, comforting Deloris.

I poked Aidan.

"Hey!" I said. "I have an idea."

I leaned over and whispered in his ear. Aidan stared at me and gave me a thumbs up.

We tugged at Ms. Spangler's arm. We told her our plan.

"Great idea, you two!" she said. "Do you need someone else to help?"

We asked Sean and Britt.

Ms. Spangler put her arm around Deloris and told her what we were doing. Deloris rubbed her eyes and stopped crying.

"Be as quick as you can," Ms. Spangler said.

The four of us hurried to the Art Room. We explained what we needed to Mr. Robinson, the art teacher. He rubbed his hands together.

"I have just what you're looking for."

He led us to an empty table and gave us colored paper, markers, glue, and scissors. Aidan drew. Sean did the cutting. Britt and I pasted. We finished lickity-quick and then looked at our project.

"High fives!" Sean said.

We hurried back to the classroom. Ms. Spangler smiled at us.

"We'll now hear our last report."

Deloris rushed over and looked at our artwork. Her smile was wide and happy.

"It's the St. Lucia flag!" she cried. "Thank you!"

Ms. Spangler bent over and put her arms around Aidan, Sean, Britt, and me.

"You four have done a wonderful job of working together to help a classmate," she said softly.

She smiled at Aidan and me.

"And I knew you two could get along if you tried."

I did a little wiggle.

"Are we Nice Mice?" Britt asked.

Ms. Spangler laughed. "Yes, you certainly are! I'm very proud of you."

Deloris and Sean stood at the front. Sean held up our colorful paper flag. Everyone *ooh*ed and *aah*ed. Deloris pointed to the blue background of the flag.

"This color stands for the sky and the Atlantic Ocean and the Caribbean Sea."

Sean pointed to the gold triangle shape in the middle.

"The color gold means sunshine."

Deloris tapped the black and white lines around the triangle.

"These two colors stand for the different races of people who live and work together on the island."

Sean pointed to the triangle.

"This shape is for the Piton mountain range."

Gilana and her mom had shiny eyes. They squeezed each other's hands. Ms. Spangler came up to the front.

"I want to add something to this wonderful report," she said. "The black and white colors in this flag also stand for getting along and working together. And today the class worked together perfectly."

She smiled at us.

"And now it's time to begin our party. As a special treat, Gilana brought in a tape of reggae music."

Everyone cheered and clapped.

"Please line up for pizza," Ms. Spangler said. "And no pushing!"

The reggae music started. It had a bouncy beat. Everyone's toes tippy-tapped.

"Gilana, get in line with Brittany and me," I said.

Gilana smiled shyly. She skipped over to us.

"Thanks for making a new flag for Sean and me," said Deloris. "But I still won and winners get to go first!"

Then she pushed in front of us!

That girl is still a pain in the brain.

I heard Aidan making monkey noises behind me. Then he gave a big burp. Sean did an even bigger one.

Britt and Gilana and I looked at one another. We burst out laughing. We linked arms and began to dance to the reggae music.

Holy *Goldy* Bananas.

We had a lot to celebrate!